Introduction

A few of the poems in this book do tend to be rather lengthy, but any of them can still be easily consumed in a few minutes at most. Also, another potential pitfall, this book might appear inconsistent because there is no common theme. But that was impossible considering that I don't write poems with uniformity in mind. They are what they are: diverse. Perhaps that could logically be considered a hedge against boredom. Perhaps not.

So let's get to the why does this book exist and why should you read it?

Many years ago I wrote poems with the intention of doing this as my life's work. What changed my mind? G.I. Gurdjieff. He convinced me that poetry was of two varieties: objective and subjective. Subjective poetry was worthless. And since I could not write objective poetry, I quit. Later on, I began again ... but only half heartedly. However, I did save the poems I wrote. Most of them are included here. Still, approximately half the poems herein were written within the last two years.

For me, many of these poems represent a lifetime of work. Does that mean you should read my poems solely to reward me for remaining erect and for merely surviving so that I can assemble these pieces of my past for the world to regard with puzzlement? Well, that would be nice; but no, that's not what I have in mind.

First of all, before I proceed with this question, I would like to introduce the poems as they appear here, edited over a period of many years.

As they present themselves collectively, and as each is launched hopefully on its journey, they now represent what I now want to communicate--no more, no less. They are the survivors.

Truth is, over the years I haven't seen many poems by contemporary poets I consider worth the time it takes to even scan them. Maybe you agree. The best poems I have seen lately have been good; but none great. The great poets are apparently long gone. The last collection of poems I would nominate as "OMG incredible!" was Ted Hughes, "Crow: From the Life and Songs of the Crow."

Most poems today read like a Hallmark card and appear as though they were composed in under 5 minutes (with 3 minutes spent gazing out the window at the neighbor's sleeping Doberman). The poems in this book are being published for the simple reason that I think they are worth reading and they make a contribution to the genre that is needed. And that is the reason I think you will enjoy reading them.

I feel there is something else that should be mentioned before we move on. Many poems today are about love: poetry sections of bookstores are full of such books, but they are clearly an embarrassment of quality when placed alongside classic authors of the genre such as Donne and Cummings. Let's face it--love sells. So do Big Macs.

Furthermore, and not accidentally, none of the poems herein have anything to say on this subject of love. Several are indeed about relationships ... but not love. And I have included no feel-good poems. When I am feeling good I don't write poetry. My intention is to invite people to think and perhaps, at the end, even to proclaim: "Wow, that poem really made me head fatter."

To that purpose, and to aid the reader, I have included a bit of information on most of the selections-- placed immediately before the respective poem and hopefully providing a bit of clarification. The ones with no introduction I consider to have no need of one.
One last aside. I spent many years living in an intentional community in Missouri. Several of the poems reflect this. But not exactly. They come from some other place. Hence the title, "Poems from a Parallel World."

Visions & Visitations

Poems from a Parallel World

Let Us Begin

"What happens when I grow tired of being me?"
inquired the cat of the clockface
staring at the face of time.

Nothing happens.

The Scarecrow

The first of the East Wind poems. I had been living in community for two years when this was written; the dream had begun to fade.

Imagine, not the world we see, but a different place, connected but distant. Two people traveling in a caravan, searching for a new home. What they find is something else, something unexpected.

A scarecrow in a field. One night, someone sets it ablaze. As they watch it twist in the flames, they contemplate where they are and what they have become.

The Scarecrow

Jehovah had driven us both across two ranges of mountains
and along the dry creekbed
we camped and carved our image in the tree,
and of this land we are its dormant kind
and in this land my thoughts are not mine;
there is nothing no solid ground
that does not yet belong to me:
I am a thin god in this world

We riddled our way here
fat thin and grasping
and with a last we digested the sun;
now we have a name to badge our hearts

Incandescent and terrible
we feel upon our memories like braille
searching out our past like a waterhole,
thickly and intermittently we converse

measuring and balancing
                                    measuring and balancing;

A gesture forlorn
rotating stiff and visible across more horizons
than we can dream:
This land is a leaden pot that holds us steady
the galaxy that which by its movement
we postulate our own

Moira

Another East Wind poem. Moira was someone I knew for a month, out for revenge. Her plan was to get drunk, pass out, then, when I had sex with her limp body, she would scream rape the next day and I would be tossed out of the community. A plan so transparent that it could not possibly succeed.

So it didn't. Yeah, she passed out; but then I fell asleep too.

Poem was written with no caps because it was a drama that doesn't deserve any: a short and small episode that seemed important at the time but now just a curiosity.

It should also be said, with a generous sop to Alethei, it didn't exactly happen like that. So this poem is more than the above. Much more dark, it is pulled from a different place, a different world, with different people.

Moira

you can decipher a fish by its shadow
on the bed
in the cold cold
you can ask in a dream if the ridge road behind you
has hoof marks warm
in the red mud;
but to ferry the nexus
with a quiver in your spine
there is time required
and sudden depth belies
a shadow of wings, for once
we believed in such things
and forged one another from tremulous dreams
to float the doorway softly
face to face
eye for eye

Ethyl Chlorine & Flo

A relationship at East Wind that never happened—never was going to happen. Move it to another reality, you get two people trying to make something work but not agreeing on what that something should be. So they sit there on a bench scowling and wondering what the hell is for dinner.

EC&F was the original title. Then I changed it to Melinda because that was her name and she was the reason the poem was written. But upon reflection I restored the original because the poem as written makes her into something she was not. She was actually a nice person.

To be honest, the title reflects more of what relationships in general were like at EW: trying to combine one volatile substance with another and wondering why the whole thing would always explode.

Ethyl Chlorine & Flo

Inside the white meat of acts
performed just for your perusal
there are more subtle barbs
astonished but for your bluntness:
taken aback upon this stumbling bereavement of form,
I forced the world to bring it forward
into the right before your eyes.

Would you have made
done with it
as we prest the remains into every metric inch
that failed to resonate,
or would you have tried to stuff even
that into the small space
we had become?

Somewhere in solid form
behind something something something else
made you look
                made us both look,
but as it sat beside and there upon
the bench by increments
all along,

It moved and became something
but we didn't.

Friends

Another poem from East Wind.

A friend affair. From another world not even close by. You greet someone as they depart; you wave goodbye when they reappear. The relationship is so distorted it makes little sense. More than that, it borders on the demonic.

Friends

Greetings come in greased packages
They slip through gesticulated fingers
And wrap your face with smiles
As you leave for Germany,
But when you return they chase
The train and wave you goodbye
While grimacing sadly at the window
Clawing at the railing
Breaking the ice
And shrieking at the disappearing cars

Twin Oaks in as Few Words as Possible

A community poem; but not about East Wind.

Saq was an unlucky dog that was grateful for what little she got.

Twin Oaks in as Few Words as Possible

Saq stayed behind the red barn

chained

Once a day she got a walk.
For years that was all she got:

a walk

once a day

Hardly anyone even knew she was there
The red barn was far away
Amazing she didn't go mad,
Amazing we didn't all go mad

chained up the way we were

The Peasant's Feast

The last of the community poems included here, and the one written most recently.

This poem is definitely from somewhere else. It reflects, for me, the death of community and all its promises, however obliquely, of utopia. The people still living there today would not see it this way, of course. Hardly matters. This is from another Earth. And this is me, not them.

The Peasant's Feast

Over there—the statues end.
And there, the garden shed face down among the stones;
pareidoliac crumbs trail along the departing rows.

There! See it before us? Hiding visibly among the dark forms—
simulacrums rage, instilling the aura of the fantastic
upon a dull and ordinary landscape:
footstep by footstep.

Approach very slowly and we shall learn of it.
As we speak aloud, our heels grind upon it; with holy
auspicions and ethereal honey we pay homage to consume it,
our flapping and infantile arms bloated from discourse,
our legs trailing along sodden floors.

Who are we and what has brought us to this?

Long ago? Yes, c'était.
We sat in the circles you see here scattered about.
With greasy hands and shapeless mouths,

[Truth is, we dressed in oily rags and awaited combustion.]

we spoke forthrightly, upfrontly, as in:

"Unto this moment we release upon the world what we construct,
dissemble, and configure."

From the stale air of desperation,
all that you see is constructed thus.

Then once upon a sabbath, we turned to dust!

Anticipating the vacuum—C'est là!—it appears among the old;
it pulled us like gold into threads
then prevailed where we could not stand;
not even for the sake of a solid axis did we
convince this rake of water to be perfect.

(continued)

And now, what is this apparition that rises before us?
Not knowing, we only propose.

"So we shall haul our carp of fish skins along the lake."

We cannot speak of it; so we announce,
even proclaim:

"At times such as these,
let us cross the river
and rest under the trees
as did our ancestors."

But they also failed as miserably as we
(as their ancestors must have).
So yes, our memories also will fail.
We don't know: we merely assume
so that we may perhaps suppose.

We attach thereby each skin to its given name.
The earth demands it, if it takes us back at all,
(and it does)
each upon each we bow yet still we
squeal loudly at the knife.

But here upon this gravel bar
we will not return;
nor any earthen memory to dim
as we are the last;
And few be here
and fewer yet to be:
Our short, humorless & difficult lives.

The Visitor

The most ambitious poem I have attempted. It is obviously narrative in structure and rather lengthy by necessity. I will just give here the barest motive that instigated its composition; otherwise it stands on its own or not at all.

I wanted to bring the characters of the Jesus story not only forward in time but also to make them something else entirely while still being recognizable—albeit only from a distance. I used Jane Roberts' theory of multiple realities from her book Seth Speaks to place them into a world very close to our own, but distorted as we view them.

A quote from Jane Roberts elucidates this idea:

"You exist in the midst of many other systems of reality, for example, but you do not perceive them. And even when some event intrudes from these systems into your own three-dimensional existence, you are not able to interpret it, for it is distorted by the very fact of entry."

The merits of Robert's theory can be debated, and I use it here merely as a useful tool.

It all begins on a homestead in Galilee.

The Visitor

Jesus ran his raft into a river
and upon it sailed as "The Starboard Rat."
Judas Arpeggio Simon
often called Pietr,
and Sister Croatia from Dalmatia,
slept blankly within the pen
often vaporizing into a glitch one horizon over.
Gazing solemnly about,
patiently throwing stone after stone into the tangible sun,
deriving each other as another evolved:
one   following   the other.

Pale of history,
no thought of afters,
she was like Enoch: not.
Because of nothing, she became nothing
and rolled toward other nothings like
a giant starfish turning the cyclone:
Invested and torn, she dragged herself ashore,
stepping lightly at the corner bistro,
staging her prayers that became
something she would play each Friday for
Castleday. He regarded her blankly.

Judas, sawing upon the piliferous Rock:
"Marry me and I shall make of thee a blind man's dream."

There—at The End: Simon:
End of all things: the bridge, the one who was is and won't be.
On occasion he would drive by in a red Mercedes,
the Colt of an ass,
but no one came out
(no one ever came out).
He mused they had something terrible against him,
something brazen on a servant's whim …
something not even strange but inevitable.
Gradually he stopped believing altogether: no grey cat on
the vinyl table,
no cup of soup the cat was not allowed
to sip. The world would not be reassembled into anything he

supposed. Twisting in the wind, impossible and
layered out like an island, discovering repeatedly
what no one else had obliged, he
composed the pale horse of his manuscript.

Arpeggio the Just, the one Jesus loved
(claimed to see it in his face);
odd moments—but when it came down to
odds and ends
(when the conversation turned upon a phrase
like those butt-ends of days past),
the door would wrench and Joseph
cursing and steaming would enter—stumbling and
belching. Everyone would laugh laugh—as a
jackass must.

Mary turned towards the end and spoke to no one,
acquiesced to smelling like the fresh oil
of her own painting, or
perhaps struck dumb
unable to compose even herself.
She realized like everyone else
Yahveh never provided.

On the last day Jesus remembered,
"Excuse me, this is my life."
and drove away in a Ford with a
pencil moustache.
After that, charity,
rumors, and a sayings mill.

"Greta, the house of this fabrication flew away
to Italy" (where it now resides)
just as the Church foretold,
landing in a parking lot in Loreto
because there was nowhere else to go.
The Holy Family ended in Jerusalem
assuming the role of Jews
but eventually the Romans came anyway
and chased everyone down an alley
yelling, "Excuse me, you can't sleep here tonight."
There was no room at the end.
But by then it hardly mattered,

as if it never had anyway.
She had been right all along:
echoes repeat indefinitely

The Shadow Boxer
(Barefoot on a Sandbar)

Is this my favorite poem in the collection? I think it is. It is very personal: The poet on his home planet.

The Shadowboxer

One begins with what one cannot say
I think about you waking up as you
I wonder if I were born again
could I get closer?
Only if I remembered another me
and I do not

There is no returning
there is only loss
and you would wake up no wiser.
I would stare through an opaque glass
and you would be no wiser

Why is it that I sleep with these tiny angels?
so much to sleep
I am wrapped up within you
there is no escape (I have tried)
I am bloody with trying

The sandbar crushes under my feet
I feel each grain again
but only obliquely
edge to edge
it will ever be so
and now the sun fading
and the bar grey now approaching slate
then charcoal as the sun sits fat at
half mast

There is no one here with me
They have all departed
better they did
as I have no conversation for them
but the tiny angels range about
smiling fixed smiles
that might be grimaces
I cannot tell
they are too distant
and the photos they take point into the sun
obscuring everything

(You recall that painting by Colette Miller—
the one that hung between the map of the Ottoman Empire
and the tiffany lamp? The one I would have given
you for Boxing Day?
Funny, I don't remember it at all.)

Should I worry about weariness?
(this time I won't)
I will speak of the softness of you
and the smell that makes me sleepy
(but I will not sleep!)

One often adopts a companion along the way
speaking with one voice and then to another
I will play amazing grace as the demons dance
and they will nod appreciatively
but they will not forgive me
and I will not ask
they will have their vengeance

There is a fog out upon the bay
where I would walk
people would say
"Hey, look at the old man
walking on the water. What an arrogant bastard."
I would count the fishes; I would say
"Fetch the nets. You will find 153 fishes give or take."
Give or take.
What would it profit me to be mistaken?
I will speak the dialect of loaves and fishes
as if I knew.
Will they listen because they must?
Yes. I believe they will.

I saw you just now
in your pale blue uniform
your face contorted
you were so young to dig so deeply
your sister not noticing
your eyes had closed
frolicking in the foreground
I do not know if you recovered
I assume you did

(Don't we all?)
And after all
this is not the age for this
this is the age that growls and spits
likely it will ever be so
The older I get the more I am aware
of the true horror of the world.

And now those distant tiny ones
fireflies at the edge of the universe:
How to tell a star from an insect
will be my last inquisition.
Then I will purchase a dowager cat
call it Effrontery
and tell it my elephant story
as it curls around my cold feet
for warmth.

Take Back What's Mine

This is a song with heavy gothic imagery. No need to say more. It speaks for itself.

Take Back What's Mine

(Song for the Myriad Placeholders)

The dancers that danced your way
Take your place in the night that knows your name
In the grace of that dull light
There's a face that you'll wear when the end is in sight
Got a right to take back what's mine

You can hold the hand of love forever
You can wear the face that love has made
In the frost and the silver mazes
You can laugh 'til the last stale traces
Got a right to take back what's mine

You can dream in a dream the love you're seeking
You can hang by your heart until it's gold
You can walk the deathless ocean
Feel the waves break you open
Got a right to take back what's mine

When it goes the soul is lost in sleeping
It leaves a face by the iron gate and the rose
There's a lord of the endless ages
A million eyes and a million faces
Got a right to take back what's mine

Goin' Under

Another song. Chorus adds nothing, so I omitted it.

The city is San Diego. I spent two unproductive and wasted years there working at various jobs, mainly temp agencies. At one point I lived in a van down by the river (uh, ocean rather). The weather was good. That's about the best thing I can say about San Diego where every day was like waking from one nightmare into another.

Goin' Under

Thin man in the doorway layin' down a spoon
Freight train shakin' in the pourin' rain
Headin' straight on for the fuse
City on the shoreline
The voices rise and fall
And I'm stuck inside this zoom lagoon
Like a tiger on a ball

The ocean moves like a heartbeat
Every head is bowed
The tide at your feet
You say life it's so sweet
Take it in, let it out

A ghost skin diver took a walk upon the sea
The lights went out, we both looked down
A vast blue fantasy

The King and Queen of This and That
They got a cabin on the Moon
A cat that sings, a jack that swings
The Earth is a toy balloon;
Drunkard on the highway, buzzard on the wing
They come and they go their faces all aglow
But to me it don't mean a thing

I carry on, I carry out
When I get to the bottom it's gone
Rain goes down through a hole in the ground
Still singin' that same old song

I guess it's just another stone to suffer
On the road to charity
I sleep on the cheap
I keep an eye on the street
But there's a fire inside of me

The Clean Minuet
(Cathy Adores a Minuet)

A mashup of "The Owl and the Pussycat" and various other nonsense verse with a nod to the Patty Duke Show.

The Clean Minuet

(Cathy Adores a Minuet)

"Let us speak bluntly,"
Sez the cat to the cataract,
"of bells and whistles
hems and hawks
blinks and nods
flatulence and flattery."

"When will this crazed coviality end?"
Marjorie of the Pen Knife inquired of the Moon:
"A bullet for your thoughts."

I once knew a Ted who played a Barker Banjo
and a brusque marquee
that resembled something akin to a slip knot.

But yonder, she said, is a finch on a leaf,
and a round robin enthrones
whatever a fool engenders.
"It's there," she said. "See it?—The Purple Pie Pat!
Listen as it sings The Forever Song:

'Everything, Everything
could be, dependent on one thing or … '"

He stopped and swung blackly at a fly,
then started anew,

"But this string about my hand?
It says nothing before not.
Nothing but a finch on a leaf."

A closet encapsulates
A carpol of diaphanous chickens,
A symbot of cardinals—all clustered about
to hear a portentous wharf rat sing, "Chances Are."
And the solemn wind.

everything you say gets unremembered
everything leaks around the edges

Who Are You, Comrad Miku?
(for Sandy)

A political poem of recent construction. Who is Little Jane? The Sandy we all know.

Who Are You, Comrad Miku?
(for Sandy)

On the banks of the Lefte River
A margay followed Marx to the linen

Little Jane
Little Jane
Where's that page you once gave me
Little Jane?

Fluid marks the farthest lark
And slips between the sheets you folded
Little Jane

Pressure builds by ones and twos
You sense for one, but one builds two
What name have you chosen this day today:
The flower or the stone?
Do you rinse your hair with rain
Little Jane
And look out the window
For more of the same?

Jale upon your schism failed
Balewood in the below vaults
Rancid charges, bloated flails
Display a landscape so departed
As to cast a gaze down upon you
Little Jane
How do you reply
When we ask for your reply?
When we ask for your reply
Will you look backwards at the sky?
And will you consider darkly
Every otter, every sound?

Where is your sense of place
Little Jane?
Do you have that in hand
Ready for our examination?
How will you reply
To our baseless questions?

You surely know this
Little Jane
I can see it in your grin
You think we don't see ...
But we do.

An old rock dove
Frozen in time
So likewise in place
But its eye still glistens
When it rains
And it rains quite often
Little Jane

Carnies

From a time long ago, but well remembered.

Carnies

I remember those dusty old dog days of summer
When a boy took a walk down a road that would take him forever
Midways cowboys carnival lights
And his friends were dreamweavers, small town believers,
Who rode the merry-go-round

But there were nights when the sky seemed so big
It was hard to believe there was a man on the Moon
So we rode on a trail of tall tales and rainbows
And we went where we went and loved what we loved
And in its time the world turned around
And I was up on a stage

Now the Earth has grown smaller but we're not much wiser
The lights of our cities you can see them halfway to Mars
We traded our dreams in on Nissans and Yugos
And our heroes are big-wheelers, give-em-hell TV preachers
And Wall Street bozos

Still I remember the nights when the world was so big
It was hard to believe there was a man on the Moon
But life comes and goes in tall tales and rainbows
And where it all comes from
where it all goes
Nobody knows

[Assorted Short Poems]

Melton in New Orleans

This is what I do
This is my job:
I pose naked
They give me cash and change
And I walk back and forth

Back and forth before the window:
Then I go away

How To Tell One Thing From Another

English is the language of peasant farmers in Essex.
King Henry beats them with a whip if they dare to dance
    or care to gaze upon the royal countenance.

French is something else entirely,
    n'est-ce pas?

Straws

There were so many last straws I don't remember
The last last straw was when you said
nobody eats fruit and lettuce together

Jim Cramer once said in a burst of candor:

"The stock market is down today
because a mouse ran down a leaf."

How Could I Not Be Happy?

How could I not be happy
when I see such smiling faces
at the window? …

staring back at me smiling
staring back at me and smiling

Don't Be Morose

Don't be morose
Said a jaybird to a post;
Said a field mouse
With his toast
(And it was such a brazen boast!):
Which of you loves me the most?

A Rugged Old Fart

I'm a rugged old fart
Said a kestrel to a tart
Is there anything you would like to say
To make me go away?

www.ingramcontent.com/pod-product-compliance
Lightning Source LLC
LaVergne TN
LVHW080628160826
845677LV00007B/1483